One day a mischievous little monkey left her mother's side in the tall trees and climbed down to explore the jungle. Two friendly humming birds watched her go.

She had not gone very far when she noticed a long furry creeper hanging down from some branches. She thought it looked just right for swinging on, so she took hold of the creeper and pulled herself into the air. The humming birds saw what she was doing and tried to warn her.

Two cheetahs jumped down from the branches. One of them growled loudly. Who would have dared to pull his tail? They looked round and saw the mischievous little monkey.

The bigger of the two cheetahs showed his strong white teeth. He growled at the little monkey and told her that cheetahs do not like to be disturbed.

The cheetah looked too big to quarrel with and so the mischievous monkey ran away as fast as she could. She ran until she came to a big lake. By the edge of the big lake she saw some logs.

She thought the logs looked just right for sitting on.
She could sit in the sun and watch the pink flamingos.
So she climbed up onto one of the logs. The humming
birds saw what she was doing and tried to warn her.

Suddenly the log began to move and an old crocodile flicked his tail and tossed the little monkey onto the ground. The crocodile looked cross because something had disturbed him. Then he saw the mischievous little monkey.

The old crocodile snapped his strong white teeth at
the little monkey and told her that crocodiles do not
like to be disturbed.

The crocodile looked too big to quarrel with and so the
mischievous monkey ran away as fast as she could.
She ran further round the lake until she came to a
large mudbank.

She thought the mudbank looked just right for climbing on. She could sit in the sun and watch the ripples on the water. So she climbed up. The hummingbirds saw what she was doing and tried to warn her.

Suddenly the mudbank began to move. A hippopotamus lifted his head and blinked. The little monkey slid off into the water. The hippopotamus looked very cross because something had disturbed him. He turned his head and saw the mischievous little monkey sitting in the water.

The hippopotamus showed his strong white teeth and told the little monkey to go away.

The hippopotamus looked too big to quarrel with and so the mischievous monkey ran away as fast as she could. She ran back towards the jungle and her home in the tall trees. On the way she passed a waterhole.

She was tired and thirsty, so she stopped by the waterhole to drink. As she drank her tail slipped into the water. After a while she felt something nibbling at her tail. What could it be? She looked round and saw a little fish.

She looked cross and told the little fish that she was a big monkey and that big monkeys do not like to be disturbed. She showed her white teeth. The little fish let go of the monkey's tail and swam away as fast as it could.

The little monkey went on through the jungle to her home in the tall trees. She felt very big and brave, as she swung from the branches. She beat her chest with one fist and sang as she went.